MR. TANEN'S

BY MARYANN COCCA-LEFFLER

Albert Whitman & Company

Morton Grove, Illinois

Maryann Cocca-Leffler has illustrated over
twenty books for children, many of which she
has written as well. She is author and
illustrator of *Missing: One Stuffed Rabbit*,
an *American Bookseller* "Pick of the Lists."
She lives in Amherst, New Hampshire,
with her husband, Eric, and their
two daughters.

Library of Congress Cataloging-in-Publication Data

Cocca-Leffler, Maryann, 1957-
Mr. Tanen's ties/written and illustrated by Maryann Cocca-Leffler.
p. cm.
Summary: Mr. Tanen, the principal at Lynnhurst Elementary
School, is well known for his colorful and unusual ties, but he
and his students are saddened when his boss orders him to
stop wearing them.
ISBN 0-8075-5301-8 (hardcover)
ISBN 0-8075-5302-6 (paperback)
[1. Neckties—Fiction. 2. School principals—Fiction.
3. Schools—Fiction.] I. Title.
PZ7.C638Mr 1999
 [E]—dc21
 98-33762
 CIP AC

10

To Mr. Tanen, crazy tie wearer and principal of the Lynnhurst Elementary School, Saugus, Massachusetts. —MCL

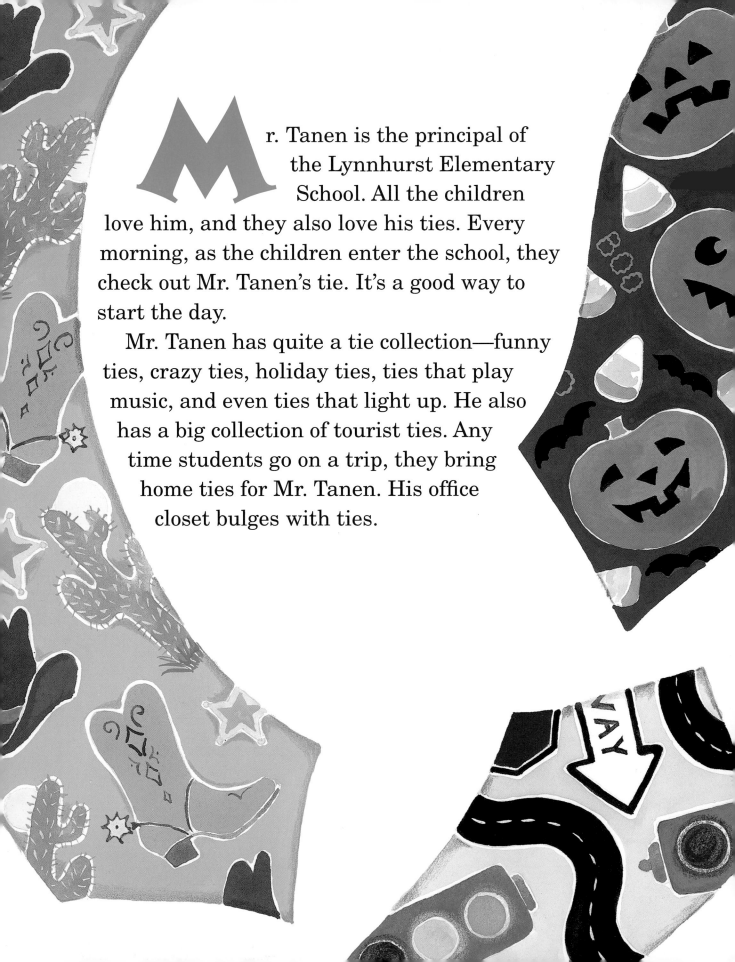

Mr. Tanen is the principal of the Lynnhurst Elementary School. All the children love him, and they also love his ties. Every morning, as the children enter the school, they check out Mr. Tanen's tie. It's a good way to start the day.

Mr. Tanen has quite a tie collection—funny ties, crazy ties, holiday ties, ties that play music, and even ties that light up. He also has a big collection of tourist ties. Any time students go on a trip, they bring home ties for Mr. Tanen. His office closet bulges with ties.

He changes his tie several times a day depending on his mood, the weather, or what's for lunch in the cafeteria.

On "Frankfurter Friday" he always puts on his Hot Dog Tie. "No one will know if I get mustard on it," he says.

If the weather suddenly changes, so does his tie. If he is wearing his Umbrella Tie, you know that it's raining even before you look outside.

And for official duties, he always wears his Red, White, and Blue Tie with yellow stars.

One day Mr. Tanen had an important
meeting with Mr. Apple at the School
Department. Everyone in town called
Mr. Apple "Mr. Crabapple" because he was
always grouchy and never smiled. Of course,
Mr. Tanen wore the appropriate tie.

"Mr. Tanen," Mr. Apple began, "you are a
fine principal. But there is one thing that
concerns me."

"What's that, Mr. Apple?" asked Mr. Tanen.

Meeting
11 am
Mr. Apple

"Education is serious business," said Mr. Apple.

"Absolutely," agreed Mr. Tanen.

"You are a role model for your students," said Mr. Apple.

Mr. Tanen nodded.

"Therefore, you should look proper at all times."

Mr. Apple pointed to Mr. Tanen's tie. "And *that* is *not* proper!"

He handed Mr. Tanen a plain blue tie.

"This is!"

"From now on, Mr. Tanen, keep your silly ties in your closet. You are to wear only blue ties."

Mr. Tanen was shocked. "No sports ties with soccer balls?"
"No."

"No tourist ties with palm trees and pink flamingos?"
"No, Mr. Tanen."

"No light-up tree ties at Christmas?"
"No, Mr. Tanen. BLUE ties— just blue."

The next day Mr. Tanen greeted the children as usual. But something was not right.

"Mr. Tanen—your tie! It's just plain blue!" said Alex.

Mr. Tanen *felt* just plain blue. He sighed. "Sorry, kids, it's 'proper' blue from now on. Strict orders from Mr. Apple."

"Boring!" said Carlo.

"How are we going to know the weather?" asked Olivia.

"Or what we're having for lunch?" said Kaylee.

Mr. Tanen shrugged sadly.

Mr. Tanen didn't feel like talking to anyone all morning.

At lunch he wished he had on his Hot Dog Tie.

When the second grade celebrated Kristin's birthday, he couldn't wear his special tie that played "Happy Birthday to You."

Alex was worried. "Mr. Tanen is not the same," he thought.

Early Monday morning the
school secretary phoned Mr. Apple.

"Sir, Mr. Tanen just called in sick. He will be out all week
with the blues. You will have to come to the Lynnhurst School
to fill in as principal."

The children were surprised to see Mr. Apple greet them
at the door. "I will be your principal for the week," he snapped.
"Let's have straight lines, no talking, no running."

"I miss Mr. Tanen already," whispered Alex.

That afternoon Mr. Apple even made recess rules. "No playing on the wet grass!" he yelled. "You'll track mud in the school!"

Recess was no fun. The kids were happy when the bell rang. As they were filing in, they saw Mr. Apple climbing a tree.

"What's he doing up there? Spying on us?" asked Kaylee.

"I can't believe it! He's bird-watching!" said Olivia.

"He actually looks happy!" said Carlo.

That gave Alex an idea.

On Tuesday Alex gave Mr. Apple a tie with birds on it.
"Thank you, Alex. But that's not quite my style."
When he was alone, Mr. Apple stared at the tie. "Cardinals
are my favorite bird," he thought. He held the tie up to his
plain gray suit. He couldn't help but try it on.

After school Mr. Apple wore his new tie to the grocery store.

"Hello, Mr. Apple," said the cashier, Miss Sweet.

"Good day," mumbled Mr. Apple.

"Lovely tie," commented Miss Sweet. "You must like birds. I'm crazy about cats."

Mr. Apple smiled a little.

On Wednesday Mr. Apple picked up his mail. Then he sat at Mr. Tanen's desk to work. But today he couldn't concentrate. He opened Mr. Tanen's closet and searched through the ties. He found just what he was looking for.

In the afternoon he went to the grocery store again.
He got in Miss Sweet's checkout line.
"Mr. Apple—now, that's a charming tie."
Mr. Apple and Miss Sweet chatted for a long time.

On Thursday after school, Mr. Apple thumbed through Mr. Tanen's ties again. This time he heard music. It was coming from a tie!

Mr. Apple headed to the grocery store.
When he got to the register, he pressed
the tie. It played "Let Me Call You
Sweetheart."

"Mr. Apple, I never knew you could
be so delightful!" said Miss Sweet.

Mr. Apple handed Miss Sweet a rose.
"Will you have dinner with me tonight?"

"I would love to, Mr. Apple!"

On Friday morning Mr. Apple greeted the children, wearing a tie with red hearts.

"Isn't that Mr. Tanen's Valentine Tie?" asked Alex.

Mr. Apple grinned. "Well, I don't think he'd mind if I borrowed it. Do you?"

"He won't mind!" shouted all the kids.

On Monday Mr. Tanen
came back to school. Mr. Apple
was waiting at the door.

"That tie, Mr. Tanen!"
grumbled Mr. Apple.

"Sorry, sir . . . got a stain on
it . . . mustard," apologized Mr.
Tanen.

"Well, it's a good thing
I bought you another one,"
said Mr. Apple. He handed
Mr. Tanen a box.

Mr. Tanen sighed. He opened the lid.

A big smile spread across his face.

"It's just your kind of blue!" said Mr. Apple.

Then Mr. Apple gave him a shopping bag filled with letters. "The kids have been writing me letters all week. They want their principal back—and so do I."

"Thank you, Mr. Apple!"

"One other thing . . . ," said Mr. Apple shyly. "Can you lend me this Wedding Bells Tie? I have an important date tonight!"